sweet, hereafter

ANGELA JOHNSON

SIMON & SCHUSTER BFYR

New York   London   Toronto   Sydney

SIMON & SCHUSTER BFYR

An imprint of Simon & Schuster Children's Publishing Division
1230 Avenue of the Americas, New York, New York 10020

SIMON & SCHUSTER BFYR is a trademark of Simon & Schuster, Inc.
For information about special discounts for bulk purchases,
please contact Simon & Schuster Special Sales at 1-866-506-1949
or business@simonandschuster.com.
The Simon & Schuster Speakers Bureau can bring authors to your live event.
For more information or to book an event,
contact the Simon & Schuster Speakers Bureau at 1-866-248-3049
or visit our website at www.simonspeakers.com.
Also available in a SIMON & SCHUSTER BFYR hardcover edition
Book design by Laurent Linn
The text for this book is set in Aldine.
Manufactured in the United States of America
First SIMON & SCHUSTER BFYR paperback edition January 2011
2 4 6 8 10 9 7 5 3

The Library of Congress has cataloged the hardcover edition as follows:
Johnson, Angela, 1961–
Sweet, hereafter / Angela Johnson. — 1st ed.
p. cm.
Summary: Sweet leaves her family and goes to live in a cabin in the woods
with the quiet but understanding Curtis, to whom she feels intensely
connected, just as he is called back to serve again in Iraq.
ISBN 978-0-689-87385-0 (hardcover)
[1. Identity—Fiction. 2. Interpersonal relations—Fiction. 3. Iraq War, 2003—
Fiction. 4. African Americans—Fiction.] I. Title.
PZ7.J629Sw 2010
[Fic]—dc22
2009027618
ISBN 978-0-689-87386-7 (pbk)
ISBN 978-1-4169-9865-5 (eBook)

For those who did and did not come home

sweet, hereafter

Prologue

THERE'S A FRONT PAGE PHOTO OF MY friend Jos standing by the side of a road on a hot summer day. I almost don't recognize him, because he's out of place. It's a frozen moment in time—but I'm so used to Jos being animated, funny and moving. It bothers me that one picture can define everything in other people's minds but never really tell the whole story.

A cop in dark shades is touching him on the arm. Gently. The photographer was close, 'cause you can see every line on the cop's and Jos's face. There weren't any lines an hour before.

. . .

It's early. Everything is quiet. Too quiet. I turn on the radio to make sure there hasn't been some kind of world-ending disaster. Hell—they do happen. More than you could ever dream they do. I've seen them, been a part of them, don't even have to watch the news to see one happening.

My feet are cool on the old hardwood floors, and I don't even mind that I'm still trying to work out a splinter. I walk to the front window.

I love the cool.

And I love the feeling I get knowing I'm walking on floors people walked on a hundred years ago. I blow the candle out 'cause finally the sun is struggling past the clouds.

The radio crackles as I stare out at Lake Erie haze.

I press my face against the window and feel cobwebs on the side of my head but don't pull back. If I listen close I can hear cars blowing past on the road about a hundred yards away.

I listen for Curtis over the drone of the radio—I do it without thinking. Then I see the groundhogs through the window and start peeling apples for them.

I do it like I breathe or walk to the sink to get a glass of water.

Automatic.

It starts to rain, and I watch like the photographer did on that burning hot summer day, while rain streaks every inch of the window.

Curtis

THERE ARE LONG ARMS ALL AROUND ME and I know I'm gonna have a serious curb put on my social life if I don't get off this couch right now and go home.

When I try to get up, Curtis's arms squeeze me more, and I know that I'm not going anywhere, not until he gives it up and lets go.

Still, I'm thinking I got so much homework I'll be up all night trying to finish it. And if I want the parents outta my business I have to keep the low B going. I ain't never been an A student, so my parents are happy about those Bs I drag out every semester.

And there's Curtis. . . .

I'd miss him if I were grounded for life. I'd

miss the way he always smells like sweet leaves underfoot in the fall. I mean, that's what I think of when I'm close to him. The woods. Leaves. Pine needles.

And the feel of his skin . . .

Shit like that. . . .

I don't say shit like that when I'm with Curtis, 'cause he doesn't swear. And even though he's never said anything when I do—I do my best not to do it in front of him.

Raised by a religious grandma is all he'll say about it.

I'm cold.

I'm cold and awake, and he's not here. No arms pull me back. I walk to the open window and smell the woods. I miss Curtis in his place on the couch beside me.

But I live here now too. So when I lean out the window to see what kind of morning sky is out there, I see Curtis, leaning against a tree. And just like that—the cold is gone.

THE DAY I LEFT HOME, MOST OF MY JEANS were in the washer, and once I was gone, I wondered what I would have to wear. If you slam the hell out of your front door, you better have your bags packed and everything you're going to need with you.

It don't look good to have to come back an hour later to get your shit.

I left home on a sunny day.

I left home on pot roast day.

I left home the day my brother scored three goals at his soccer match.

I left home the day our neighbor's cat got stuck up a tree.

I left home the day I couldn't find my house keys.

I left home the day the mailman delivered about a thousand catalogues.

I left home the day I accidentally broke my favorite CD.

I left home the day I couldn't think of a good reason to stay. I left home, and two days later nobody came for me, so I stayed where I was.

Which is here, in the woods in an old cabin surrounded by trees, bushes, and things that look harmless in the daytime but scratch the door in the night.

I left home, and Curtis told me to come right on in and stay until I was happy not to stay.

The day I left home, I had to go back for my jeans, but I didn't have to go in. They were waiting for me folded in a box outside the front door.

Curtis doesn't talk much. Some days he hardly speaks at all. In the end he tells me what he needs to tell me by smiles, touches, or the tilt of his head. I don't mind. I love the quiet. I love his quiet.

I like living here in the cabin with him, and I know he wants me here. I walk through the

ANGELA JOHNSON

cabin and touch the books that are lined against the wall. And there's just enough to remind me of him every day—just enough. Just enough to make you comfortable, but not enough to tell you too much about Curtis. And I didn't know that when I walked in the door, but that's the way it stayed.

I just know him—enough.

And that's okay, 'cause most people only know me enough. My own family only knew parts of me. My friend Marley knew a few parts. I've had secret parts of me since I was little. I'm used to it, and I guess it makes sense I'd love the secret parts of another.

THE BOARD SAYS IN PINK CHALK—

THE REVOLUTION WILL
NOT BE TELEVISED—SO
READ A FUCKING BOOK.

Ms. Jameson is way mad.

And everybody thinks they know who did it. So we all sit around with stupid looks on our faces glancing toward the back of the room at Carl.

AGB. Angry Goth Boy.

Black nail polish—kicked out for two weeks for turning over desks and screaming "fascist" at the art teacher when she was talking about the Impressionists.

Now I remember why I decided to take up merchandising and not be held hostage in rooms with thirty other people five days a week.

Ms. Jameson puts the evil eye on Carl.

He smirks at her.

I like Carl, though. We used to skip class together, back in middle school.

"So who will start today?" she says.

I don't remember too much after that until somebody taps me on my back and I jump.

Brodie.

"Was I snoring?"

Brodie starts to laugh. Even though I haven't turned around, I'd know that laugh anywhere. He can't ever hold it in, and I can't count how many times we've gotten busted because of that laugh.

"Brodie!"

"Sorry, Ms. Jameson."

And I go back to sleep and start to dream again. This time I know I'm dreaming. I'm sitting on the side of the road and it's raining. I've always loved being in the rain. Now a man that I realize I should know but can't remember his name walks up to me. It could be Jos or even my brother. In my dream the familiarity is just there. I can't tell if his face is wet because of the rain or because of the tears. And even in my dream all I want to do while I'm sitting there is to go after the photographer and beat the hell out of her for freezing this man's crying face in my mind. But it's just a dream.

I walk out of school with Brodie and try to remember how we came to be friends. He's a jock, class president, and dates cheerleaders— but he's funny, kinda twisted, and mad smart. And I'm pretty sure the class president thing was just so he could get snack machines in the senior lounge.

"I need a ride," he says.

"Alice is funny about who she gives rides to. Last time you were in her, there was that thing . . . "

"Dag, Sweet. All I did was change the radio a few times and mess with the heat. That shouldn't make a truck stall."

Brodie busts open a bag of chips and laughs while throwing some at three sophomore girls walking by. They laugh and scream his name.

"Cute." I pull Alice out of the parking lot.

"I know," he says.

"Where do you need to go, then?"

"I don't know—just drive. Or we could go get food. There's only so many chips I can eat before I start to starve to death."

I slow down for a dog crossing the road.

"Snack machines not working out so hot, huh?"

Brodie turns and looks at me like I just went through his underwear drawer. Then he looks hurt. I laugh. Then I remember it's the reason I introduced Brodie to my friend Jos: Sometimes they're both just too much fun and full of shit. They play well together and make me laugh.

"C'mon, Brodie—class president? You'd rather be watching football or some crazy cartoon with people as underwater creatures or dogs and cats playing saxophones . . ."

"Yeah, okay, that's me."

"Yeah, but why don't most people know that about you?"

"You do. But that's who you are," he says.

"What do you mean, that's who I am?"

Brodie finishes up the chips and sticks the empty in his courier bag.

"Yo, Sweet, have you ever really looked at yourself in a mirror?"

"Where you going with this—way to get the subject off of you, huh?"

Brodie smiles. "If you ever even acted like you would look at somebody from this school, there'd be a riot. Man, everybody would be creeping around your locker—stalking you.

I don't know what the problem is, 'cause at first like any dumbass guy who gets viciously rebuffed by a mommy, I wanted to believe you just liked girls."

"I do like girls—"

Brodie smacks me with a balled-up bandana he finds on the seat next to him. "You know what I mean. Anyway, whatshisname is lucky."

"His name is Curtis."

Brodie laughs, then hangs out the window and hollers something to a passing car. I pull off the road into the parking lot of Tony's Café.

Me and Brodie jump out the car and head inside. I think about locking Alice but decide not to. Brodie is about four steps ahead of me when he shifts the bag on his shoulder and a box of pink chalk falls out.

4

THERE'S A BIG SUGAR MAPLE TREE THAT sits in the corner of the yard. I sometimes lean against it and fall asleep. Curtis always asks me why I'm leaning against myself.

In this cabin with Curtis I wake up to the sound of the wind. Or an animal running underneath the house. Groundhogs have moved in. Well, they've probably always been there.

Curtis likes them.

He calls them the wild pigs and leaves them vegetable scraps and tells me that they like salsa music. He says that he plays salsa music to the groundhogs. Then they come and hang out in the front yard.

I thought he was making it up.

So one day I'm leaning against the tree and there's salsa music coming from the window— and there they were. Three groundhogs sitting and chewing. I sat and watched them for a long time, until it started getting cold. But just when I thought about going back in, Curtis came out the door dressed in camouflage and carrying an old canvas jacket.

He knelt down and wrapped me up in it.

Then he sat down and wrapped his arms around me.

Reason six hundred and ninety-two why nothing should shock me but it always does.

Where we live there is nothing strange about men in full camouflage. You see that stuff in the woods, in the supermarkets, and going down the back roads with gun racks and pickups. I never did understand it. Got used to it, but never understood it. But I still wanted to know why he was covered in the gear.

He could read me.

"I'm in the reserves. Already been to Iraq— probably have to go back."

Curtis took out apple pieces and threw them to the groundhogs.

"You mean the army? I mean, I can get with them when they're rescuing people and shit."

"We do that."

"Did you ever shoot your gun?"

"Weapon," he said.

Curtis threw more apples to the hogs—who now were seriously eating.

"But you're going to college. Why are you in the reserves?"

Curtis frowned and kept pitching apples.

"It's helping me pay. I got this cabin and my car. That's it. I can't sell the cabin. It came from family. It's mine, but I could never sell it. So it's the reserves."

"I thought you were nonviolent, a pacifist. You look sick every time you read about someone getting shot."

Curtis frowned again and said, "They might be coming for me—any day now. Any day."

He leaned against me again and kissed the back of my neck.

"If you've already been, why do you have to go back? I mean, damn it, you got responsibilities. You have to feed the wild pigs. Give them the money back and get a job on campus."

The groundhogs looked up at me like they were thinking, *YOU ARE SUCH A BIG-ASSED LIAR. IT'S ALL ABOUT YOU?*

They were right.

. . .

A story Curtis tells.

When he was little, there were always cousins that lived with his family. Sometimes there were as many as thirteen kids in their house. It never mattered. They got by. When his parents were alive, they made a lot of money and believed in sharing everything with everybody.

He was six years old when one of his cousins got sick and had to go to the hospital. She never came back. But because he was only six, the older kids told him she wouldn't be back because a dragon got her. He liked fairy tales, and they thought he would understand.

They didn't let the little kids go to the funeral.

So he stayed home and started going through all his books. Afterward, when the family went to malls, he'd always want to go to the bookstore. He was looking. . . . He was looking in all the fairy tales that had dragons in them. He was looking for his cousin. He expected her to appear in the window of a castle. Or maybe she would be running across a moat. But the girls never looked like his cousin.

They were pale, blond, and looked like teenagers.

His cousin was chocolate-skinned, had black plaits, and was five.

He never found her.

The dragon had taken her a long way away and for good.

5

I WATCH THE TELEVISION IN THE FRONT window of Morry's Electronics. The flat screen is so big it takes up the whole window. I blow cigarette smoke over my shoulder. A few minutes ago Jos told me I smelled like a smokestack. That's why I try not to get too many fumes on me.

I'm not as into the TV as I'm into what's on it.

There's long lines of troops coming out of a hangar onto a runway. And if you don't look at their faces, you don't see that most of them are so young it's probably the first time a lot of them have ever left their state, let alone the country.

My dad said the fatigues are different than when he was in Vietnam, 'cause they were in a jungle. The colors now are better for the desert.

The farm kids are the same as they were when my dad went to Vietnam. The city kids have that walk . . . like they know where they're going.

I know somebody like that. He walks ahead, sure of himself, and never acts like he doesn't know where he's going. He moves like he was here and did everything before people even walked the planet. He's that comfortable in his skin.

His skin. His skin.

I put my cigarette out and watch as boys and girls, men and women, fill up a whole transport plane, and I feel cold. After a few minutes a woman with a stroller is standing next to me. She watches the TV and moves the stroller back and forth. The baby starts to babble, but in a minute it's asleep.

"I'm so proud," the woman says, her eyes filling up with water. I feel bad for her. I look at her baby and figure her husband or somebody real close to her is going to fight or is already there. I figure she feels sick with worry every day.

"Is someone in your family over there?" I ask.

She keeps moving the stroller and looking at the baby. "Oh, God, no!" she says. "I don't really know anybody in the military. . . ."

She smiles.

I stop watching the TV and look at the baby. And hell, I know this kid already has a college fund. His mom's eyes shine, and I realize she looks like she just stepped out of a spa.

Her skin glows, and she smells like apples in her hooded yellow top and white yoga pants. Her wedge-cut hair catches a breeze. Her diamond tennis bracelet sparkles when she brushes an imaginary hair off her cheek.

And why did she say, "God, no!"? I betcha there's some accountants and doctors over there who had to go into the reserves to pay for their degrees.

She keeps talking.

"I'm proud because we know our safety is at stake, and—well, we really do need to bring these people down. . . ."

I start to light another cigarette but remember the baby and slide the pack back into my jeans.

"What people?"

The woman looks at me the way people look

at children they think are stupid and uncared for—with a mixture of *The schools have failed us* and *I wonder if this child's parents know anything*.

"Those people."

"Who?" I say.

The woman starts to look me over. Black girl, five feet six, curly 'fro, jeans, and T-shirt with dogs on it that says I'M ONLY IN IT FOR THE PUGS.

"Oh, honey . . . You're too young to understand, I guess."

She looks like she wants me to understand. She really does. But she doesn't get how dumb she sounds with those words coming out of her well-made-up lips. I want her to go away. I want her to go back to her well-fucking-appointed house and shut up. I want her to not have an opinion that is not mine. I want her to be somebody else who walked up to this window and talked about how bad and hopeless this all is. I want her to be anybody else but who she is.

I want her to ask me if I know somebody over there.

Then again—no—I don't want her to ask that. She's not special enough to know. I close my eyes and wish her away.

When I open them again, she's still there, so I say—

"All I know is those people never follow me in stores to make sure I'm not stealing, those people don't pull me over for no good reason when I'm driving, and other than that I know about as much about those people as you do about them."

That got rid of her. . . .

In five seconds the woman is moving away from me down the sidewalk and pushing the stroller toward the baby boutique. The kid wakes up, screaming. And I wonder if she would be so damned sure about bombs and guns if her child was running through the desert trying to stay alive.

I pull out my pack from my jeans, light up another cigarette, and finish watching as the talking head smiles her stupid smile and talks about how the army and marines do a great job. I want to grab her through the TV, shake her, tell her to stop reading the script and think for herself.

The army and marines would rock so much better with their asses back here at home.

ANGELA JOHNSON

How I met Curtis.

Curtis has the darkest eyes. Clear and shining. His eyes are like the girl with the wings, but longing. I met her before I met him. I'd seen his eyes way before I started working in my friend Jos's store. Even though technically that's where I first met him.

I knew his eyes.

Then he smiled at me.

Okay, I thought I knew him as he wandered around the store touching some things and laughing at others. (That Santa with his pants falling down was pretty stupid.) But when he took a pair of silvery wings down from the wall—it was like I'd known him for a long time. And then I knew him. His eyes used to live next door to me.

I used to live on lockdown. It was always for something so minor I couldn't remember what I did a few hours later, but in hindsight know I probably did it. I did what I always did when the parental popo nabbed me. I sneaked out of the house to sit in the backyard, 'cause I was in lockdown—a lot. And I sneaked out—a lot. After a while it was almost like a game. For me, anyway. My parents just gave up thinking they could keep me jailed in my room. And I just did what I did.

I used to watch our next-door neighbor from my lawn chair.

I started noticing the Wing Girl, 'cause she never left the yard. I figure she was probably in her mid-twenties. She had some teenaged brothers and sisters who were older than me, but they all went to JFK, the Catholic high school, and never hung out with anybody in the neighborhood.

She got mailed wings through the UPS. And one day, when she opened them, they fell out from some sparkling green tissue paper shimmering and ready to tie onto her back.

And I didn't know then (like I didn't know her name) that there would be a story about her and the wings.

Everybody's got a story.

So I'd sneaked out again to sit in the back-yard, knowing that it was time for the wings.

The only thing that divided our yards were two rose of Sharon trees. And in a few minutes she was out back—big 'fro, bare feet, jeans, and an old T-shirt—unwrapping her wings. She was about ten feet from me, but it didn't look like she knew I was there.

Her new wings were green with yellow and orange butterflies.

She put them on and walked across the yard like she always did. I stood up and watched her. The wing thing was in then—but she was pushing the age limit. Even so, I was drawn to the smile on her face. I thought she might just take off and fly over Heaven.

She walked up and back across the lawn, until after a few minutes one of her brothers came out, took her by the arm, and started to lead her in. She let him. Before he walked away, he turned and stared at me for almost a minute with the darkest eyes I'd ever seen.

. . .

Now here comes the stupid thing. I wanted those wings.

I wanted to sail around my backyard, wings ready to fly me anywhere. I wanted to be the girl over five who could wear wings and have everybody believe it. You know—magical and dreaming of sprites and troll kings. There were a couple of girls I knew who could carry it off. And damn—there was the woman next door.

I wanted not to be of the earth.

I wanted to be winging around in the sky.

A couple of weeks later I took the package from her porch before she could get to it. I saw that the wings came from some shop in New Orleans. The box felt empty.

Stupid, but I wanted them.

I wanted to be as happy as she looked in her wings, but just as I was about to jack the wings, she came out on her porch. She walked out and smiled at me. Just smiled. Then I saw what it was about her. She had an old gash that went from her cheek, up her forehead, on into her hairline. Her eyes were faraway and unfocused.

It wasn't the wings.

I handed her the box.

The rest of the summer was messed up and

boring except for the few times when my girl Marley and Bobby busted me out.

But by the end of the summer the Wing Girl and her brothers and sisters were gone. I missed her walking back and forth. Winged and ready to fly.

A couple of years later Curtis walked into the store. When I saw him and looked into his eyes, I saw her eyes—the girl with the wings. He strolled around the store, looking for wings to send to her. His face was kind, and he had his sister's eyes, but they twinkled.

7

CURTIS AND ME STAY UP ALL NIGHT LONG and listen to the water crash against the beach up at Mentor-on-the-Lake. We camp next to the bikers and their families having bonfire cookouts and staying in the cabins all over the woods by Lake Erie.

We usually bring burritos from Taco Tantos and warm 'em up on somebody's fire.

No problem.

Sometimes when it gets real quiet, I think I hear him calling over to someone on the dark beach to turn the music up. He does that. He doesn't care what kind of music it is; he just thinks it should be loud.

And whoever is playing it always turns it up.

I drive up my old street, real slow, and I think I can do it this time. I can turn in to the driveway, turn the truck off, open the door, and get out.

It's okay if I stand by the truck for a few minutes.

It's okay if I think about it for a while too, I don't have to go up to the door like I'm being chased by something. I can take my time.

I can look at the perfect grass.

I can count the petals on the perfect rose bushes.

I can see my reflection in the sparkling front windows.

I can stand and wait before I knock on the door. I won't go running in. I want them to know that I miss them but can do all right without them. I want them to smile when they answer the door and not get that look that says—*What the hell is it?*

I want them to ask me where I've been and if I'm getting enough to eat and am I in a good place. I want them to take me in their damned perfect house and sit me down on the couch and tell me they made pie. Or even bought pie just for me.

I want to be asked to stay to dinner (I always

wanted to have dessert before dinner in that house). And if somebody asked me to play piano—I would. Even if I haven't played for anyone in ten years and used to slam out of the house if anybody said anything about it.

I'd play.

And after all of that if somebody asked me to stay the night, at first I'd say no. I can't. Got something to do and somebody would miss me. I promised a friend. I've got to get up real early the next morning. Or even I don't want to put anybody out.

But maybe my room is now that office my dad always wanted. And maybe I won't get to listen to his story about being so poor when he was little they picked dandelions in the park to eat.

But I would.

I'd listen.

In the end Alice and me roll on by the empty driveway and dark house that used to be my home. I turn the music up, 'cause that's the way it should be, and head back to Curtis and the cabin with a smile on my face.

8

EVEN THOUGH IT'S RAINING AND LOOKS like everything might be flooding, I go for a walk down by the river. It runs about fifty feet behind the cabin. I like to watch the fish. I can sit there for hours.

Most days are so quiet here.

Sometimes here in this cabin I have to turn the volume on the radio-CD player up to the point of me getting a headache to keep it all together. Too much quiet. I don't know anybody who lives in the quiet like me. It would drive my friends crazy. So I don't ask them over.

But that's not the only reason. There are other things.

I got no iPod.

No TV.

No computer.

But there's books lined up and down the walls on bookshelves Curtis built himself from some trees in the woods.

When everybody found out I had left home, it didn't seem to be any big thing. I think they wondered why it took me so long to leave or why my parents took so long to kick my ass out. But when they found out about Curtis—everybody started talking.

You know people always think it's about sex. Everybody is too hooked up on who's doing what to who. And most people were wondering who my who was. Only my friends didn't care that I didn't hook up. But like Brodie said, it makes you dangerous. People can't put you in a box.

I'm not dangerous.

I wore knee-high rain boots and white lipstick for years. Didn't bother me, but I think it pissed people off. I still don't understand. These days it pisses them off that I go to parties and hang but not at school.

I guess most people are like—how the hell did she get here? And who is she? But I always get invited. I always have fun, so even when I'm leaving school for the woods somebody usually yells across the quad—"PARTY TONIGHT, SHOOGY!"

And I drive Alice and probably pick up about five or six people who sit in the back of the truck and ride to some loud-assed party with too much beer in the middle of a field or some rich kid's house whose parents are gone. Me and Brodie usually end up standing around and bitching and complaining about nothing in particular and everything in between.

I sit by the creek after coming out of the woods and only notice that I'm soaked through when I stand up and feel the water run down my legs. I walk, dripping, through the green leaves, stepping over branches, and I watch where I'm going so I don't fall in animal holes or break an ankle on hidden rocks. But I know the way back to the cabin with my eyes closed.

I walk down the path and climb the six steps.

I start stripping everything as soon as I'm inside. I drop my shoes and shirt by the front door, my shorts by the couch, my bra by the bathroom door, and my panties in front of the tub.

I run hot water into the tub as I stare out

the big window above me. With the stone floors and tree brushing against the window, it's like bathing in the woods.

The big claw-foot tub makes up for no iPod, no TV, no people around. I climb in and sink down up to my chin, and that's when I know I've been walking around freezing. The heat feels good. I start to warm up.

There's still enough light to read when I reach for the book I've been keeping on the floor by the tub. It's a story about a girl who takes care of her brother while being haunted by the ghost of a long-dead uncle. And I keep reading till the trees beside the window are hushed but still wet and have blocked out the little bit of sun left.

A FEW THINGS ABOUT CURTIS . . .

He loves dogs.

He's six feet two.

Never swears.

He hardly eats meat but loves fish.

Loves hip-hop, jazz, baroque, bluegrass . . .

Has seven brothers and sisters.

Has been to Iraq once and doesn't want to go back and doesn't want to talk about it.

His sister Sadie, the Wing Girl, is the oldest child.

He slammed poetry for a few years.

Loves silent movies.

Can recite whole parts of James Baldwin's books.

Was picked up by cops once when he was seventeen 'cause he was in the "wrong" neighborhood.

Isn't bitter, but doesn't trust like he used to.

Is three years older than me.

Didn't say no when I showed up with my box of jeans.

Curtis walks off into the dark of the night, and it's usually after a real bad dream. I hear him cross the floor, pull on clothes and shoes, then disappear out of the room, then out of the little cabin. And for a few days afterward he hardly speaks.

It ain't that he's mad at me—I can tell. He smiles, does what he has to do, and listens to me when I'm talking. But it's like something took his voice away. After a few days his voice comes back. I don't say a word. I don't ask where he goes or ask why he's not talking, 'cause sometimes you almost don't want to know the answer to some things.

I couldn't give an answer to my parents when they asked me why I disappeared for a week last year in my truck.

I couldn't tell them that it was just a long

long end to not ever feeling like I was one of them. How do you tell people who love you that? How do you tell them you spent much of your life looking around the rooms of your house and not finding much that might keep you there?

I ain't mad anymore. It doesn't do any good.

But after I left the first time, I knew that was the beginning of the end of my life with my family. I'd spent the days I was gone at the lake or at the Cedar Lee watching art films. I spent a whole two days watching opera on the screen in high def. I love opera now right alongside Jay-Z.

I gave a ride to a woman named Jodie and her little girl Maddie who were broken down on the side of the road. Jodie's cell phone was dead and her little girl (dressed in a tutu and a Cleveland Browns jacket) was late for her recital. I took them to the high school where the recital was taking place. Hundreds of little girls and boys in dance clothes ran, danced, and hopped into the building.

Jodie thanked me for the ride and for letting her use my cell phone (which I'd turned off days before so I didn't have to listen to my parents calling me every few minutes asking me to come home). The recital had been more important than staying with her car until her husband got there. I liked that.

Maddie sang the whole way and was singing when they both got out of the truck and joined the hordes. I thought of my mom. But I still didn't go home.

I spent a few days with Bobby and Feather. Feather would wake me up with toast and shoes in her hands.

We took walks into their backyard and the woods beyond it. Her hand was warm as she held on to mine and pointed out squirrels, birds, and wildflowers. Her curly black hair was wild on her head as she ran past me to find something new under a tree.

Bobby didn't question me as he made the couch up for me to sleep. We just stayed up late talking about nothing. But once, just once, he wanted an answer to something I didn't have an answer to.

"What do you feel connected to, Sweet?"

I sat there surrounded by his canvases and pictures of his family back in New York, Feather's picture books and little-girl toys poking out everywhere. I knew what he was connected to. And he was connected without pain.

ANGELA JOHNSON

I couldn't answer the question. I just leaned against him and read him one of Feather's books.

And when I finally went home—I still couldn't tell them why I left. And there was no way I could tell them that even though I was sleeping in my own bed again, I was already gone.

10

IF YOU TELL A SECRET, IT'S OUT IN THE world forever. You can't ever take it back or explain to the person whose secret it was why you gave it up.

If you don't tell a secret, my mom says it's like living in a little bit of hell—forever.

But I don't believe in hell.

At least not the one the pastor in my old church talked about.

I do have secrets.

But maybe it's not a secret at all. Maybe I could always see it in his eyes. Feel it when he was with me one minute and gone the next minute even when I still held him beside me.

So it's best not to tell.

For now.

I asked Jos once what he was doing in a boring little place like Heaven. He smiled.

He said, "I love my strange mother, I guess."

I understood that. Maybe if my own mother was a little stranger and not so upright I wouldn't have wanted to leave her either. But she was a little stiff, well, a whole lotta stiff, and I didn't think I could feel for her what Jos felt for his mom. It was sad, but that was that.

It was so sad me and Jos decided to drive into the city and go to a psychic advisor on the west side near a deserted mill. We'd gotten her number from the *Free Times* beside an ad that said someone needed a part-time gardener and bird sitter.

Her house sat at the end of a pink flamingo and wooly sheep kind of street. All the houses looked like Hansel and Gretel might visit them for something good to eat. We parked behind an SUV with a moon and star painted on the back door. We walked up the steps and were met by a black and white cat that rolled on its back for attention.

I sneezed and smiled. Jos scratched the cat on the tummy and didn't even get clawed.

Then a woman in a white, blue, and peach

jogging outfit came to the door. Jos laughed. Her name was Magda, her hair was blue and purple, and she said she was ninety-six years old. She gave us tea from Botswana in her overcrowded living room. She smelled like roses.

And a few minutes later she was holding Jos's hand so tight he said later he thought she was going to pull it off his arm. She told Jos soon he'd understand more of the world than he wanted to.

She told me that I was destined to come and go.

It was dark and raining when we left her house. The old mill just a ghost shadow in the distance. We realized we'd been there for over three hours talking to Magda—but I swear those are the only two things either of us can remember her saying. We try to remember but can't.

We left the city and drove the hour or so back to Heaven, only talking to each other when a commercial came on the radio. Jos with a sore hand and me with the knowledge that I'd probably never stay still in the world.

11

MARLEY HANGS OUT ALICE'S PASSENGER
window and only puts her head in long enough
to ask, "You smokin' anymore, girl?"

I feel the pack in the back of my jeans. If
I was any kind of girl, I'd have some kind of
purse with about fifty thousand things in it, and
I could lie.

"Trying."

"I blame your mom."

I say—"You think she intentionally wanted
me to catch her nasty habit?"

"I've seen it before. Bonding. Maybe she
wanted you two to have something in com-
mon."

I look at her like she's crazy.

"Scratch that."

She lays her head on the open window as we fly down the road toward the lake to get us a good spot before people with suntan lotion and beach toys and their jelly-faced kids take up the whole sand trap.

It's spring break and stupid hot for late March.

But it's Ohio. Tomorrow it could be snowing, so you got to grab what you can in the time it's given to you. In a few minutes Alice has slowed down, and we're in line with about a few hundred other cars.

Marley looks at me, and I know we didn't leave early enough. We turn the radio up and inch along for about twenty more minutes until I see somebody selling barbecue on the side of the road. We pull over.

We sit on top of Alice and eat sausage po'boys as the traffic keeps crawling.

We see some people from Heaven and wave and point and laugh at them for being where we were a little while ago. After throwing down two po'boys each we hang out with the barbecue man and talk about summer. He's short and round with a soft voice. He waves toward a travel trailer parked nearby when he needs something. Then one of his grandkids comes out and gives him more sauce, vinegar, and water or whatever.

Me and Marley talk with Chuck until the traffic speeds up. But we know the beach is packed.

Chuck waves us away with po'boys to go and a couple of bags of chips.

We head back home but have to stop the truck on the side of Route 306 to get out and dance to a song we'd been whining that we hadn't heard on the radio the whole day.

After that we're okay with everything.

I drive for the woods.

"Let's hang out on the porch and count the groundhogs," Marley says.

I laugh and nod my head. Hell, it beats jelly-faced, sticky, sunblocked kids walking all over you.

I'm pulling up into the long driveway when I see a car about thirty feet in front of me. I have to brake fast, 'cause I'm used to flying up the drive. Nobody but me ever uses it.

Two men in uniforms are knocking on the front door.

Marley says, "What's up—you join up and not tell me?"

A cool breeze breaks through the heat and freezes me to Alice's seat. I see that Curtis isn't home yet. After the two men talk to me, I'm glad he's not home. Curtis is AWOL, and it would have been a long-assed time before I saw him again. He would have been arrested at the door. A few minutes later I swear I see Curtis leaning against a tree out back. But I blink, and he's gone.

Swimming the Pacific

12

ONCE MY GIRL MARLEY COUNTED THE steps from her house to Ma's Superette. I guess we didn't have that much to do back then. Why else would she need to actually count the footsteps to a place we practically lived? She says she doesn't remember how many steps there were, but she wrote it down somewhere.

Now when I drive past Ma's, I only stop at Marley's and remember the steps I used to take when the center of town was our whole lives.

Now I watch from my truck as screaming little kids swoop down the slide on the playground in the middle of town.

Now I roll past my parents' house, always slow down just as I come to the driveway—but never stop.

I put my cigarette out in the ashtray and swear it's the last one I'll ever smoke. Until the next time, I guess. Then I pull my truck Alice over and jump out just as a school bus flies by. My stomach catches for a second, but I keep walking across the street.

I creep into the shop. Nelly's rapping on the radio, and there's too much orange air freshener smelling up the place.

"What's up, girl?"

"Nothing."

"Glad you've decided to come to work. You know those people from the state do actually show up here sometimes to check on you."

Jos has got his feet up on the cash register in his go-to-work, play, everyday jeans and a T-shirt that says STUPOR. I smile and go into the back of the store and start opening boxes. Late again, and he still hasn't fired me, 'cause he knows what that would mean. For me, school. For him, not getting cheap labor.

For true Jos is all right. He's letting me do the vocational thing here, and that's okay by me, 'cause I only have two classes a day, and that's about all I can stand.

Jos really doesn't need to worry, because ain't nobody from school's gonna push it. That would mean me in class full time, and nobody wants that. I know the school doesn't—and I'm in agreement.

I keep unpacking boxes as Jos sets a cup of coffee beside my foot and goes back to the front of the store to answer the phone.

After a while I've unpacked a box of candles, two boxes of fairy wings—a sure sign of Halloween coming—and some throws that are the softest things I ever felt. Before I know it, I'm wrapped up in a gray one, sitting in the back room, missing the warmth of Curtis's skin, and wanting a cigarette.

And the funny thing is, I just saw him thirty minutes ago.

But things have been sliding somewhere dark since the army reserves showed up looking for him.

He never said a word, and I didn't tell him. The groundhogs got his attention for the rest of the night.

And I know something. I know the feeling, 'cause it's not too long since I had it myself. I think Curtis is already gone. Back to Iraq or wherever. He's slipping away—quietly, as usual.

"I USED TO WATCH THE NEWS, BUT IT WAS always changing, and I could never follow the story."

Quote from a lady on a bus I once rode to Cincinnati.

IF I THOUGHT IT WOULD DO ANY GOOD,
I'd lay on my horn until the person who boxed
me in looks out a store window and decides to
come move their ride. But I know I won't be
getting out anytime soon, so I climb on top of
my truck, light up, and lie on the hood looking
up at the clouds.

In a minute warm hands are running up my
bare legs, tickling them.

The hands take my cigarette, put it out
against a telephone pole by the car, then throw
it in the storm sewer since there's no trash can
nearby.

"Damn—can't I even have a bad habit?"

"You got more than anybody I know."

Marley's little brother, Butchy, climbs up next to me.

"What up?" he asks.

I miss my cigarette but don't light up another. I want Butchy to stay and hang for a while. At least lie on the old hoopty with me so I don't look like a stone-cold lone loser.

I smile at him.

"Yo—again, what are we doing stretched out on your ride?"

"Stupid parker," I finally say.

Butchy sits up to look at the brand-new car wedged up against Alice, then lies back beside me.

"Remember Mike Boyd's cousin Darnell?"

"Yeah, he was funny as hell that summer he stayed with Mike and we all hung out. He's crazy fun."

"You know he got shipped out."

I feel a twinge in my stomach.

Butchy looks up. "He got hurt. He was on patrol, and his carrier ran over an IED. They say he'll be home soon."

I don't know how long we lie there watching clouds blow by and listening to people calling out to each other. It seems like a whole day, 'cause we don't talk, and it's the best afternoon I've had in a long time.

The bank is closing when a man in a suit, dragging files on luggage wheels, looks over at us and gets in the car that's held me hostage for hours. Because I didn't have anywhere else to be, I wave to him, then blow a kiss.

Butchy laughs so hard he almost rolls off the truck.

When Alice is free, Butchy jumps down, ready to go. He looks down the street, then at me.

"It's pretty bad about Darnell, huh?"

I nod my head and look up the street too.

Then Butchy leaves, and the clouds cover the sun again, and there's nobody on the street anymore. I can even hear the signal light clicking the change from yellow to red.

And it's true I got nothing to do and no place to go in a hurry.

I look across the street to Ma's Superette and put my keys in my pocket. Haven't been in Ma's in a long time. . . . But just as I get to the door, I get a real warm feeling. When I look in and see the barrel of flip-flops and bin of beach toys, I turn back.

I look down at my hiking boots and start walking and counting steps from Ma's Superette to my parents' house, and I think about a boy I only knew one summer.

15

CURTIS FOUND A LETTER OUT BY THE dump one day when we went for a walk. Curtis saw the letter fluttering in the wind, leaned down, and picked it up.

I don't think I ever heard him laugh so hard. He kept the letter in his wallet. Now it's in my back pocket. I wanna remember that day and the way we both laughed.

Grace,

I have been thinking of you for so very long. It's sad to me that things have not worked out for us. I had dreams that we would be together forever. I never thought it all would end so quickly or hurt so deeply. I blame myself.

I should not have let others be more important than you. Truly I don't think I ever realized how wonderful you were. Yes, I was hurt when you burned my garage down with my two cars in it. Yes, I was surprised when I went to the bank and you had cleaned out the savings account.

And yes, I know people in the neighborhood must have been talking about how you threw all my clothes out the front door, drove to Harry Fuel and Eats for a can of gas, and lit everything on fire. And most definitely, my family will never invite you to another get-together (me either, I guess) after you told everybody (in detail) the little things I say about them to make fun.

But Grace, I forgive you everything—if you'll just come back to me and Buddy (who no longer tries to bite me like you trained him to).

Love,

John

By the time Jos finishes reading the letter, me and Brodie are almost crying in pain from laughing. I try to take another sip of lemonade and stretch out on the lounge chair.

We're sitting in Jos's backyard surrounded by ugly yard crap. His mom collects it. So we sit pretending we're on a beach in Hawaii, chillin' with wooly sheep and little Dutch girls. And one of those shadow men who lean against trees—just creepy.

We have the backyard to ourselves 'cause Jos says his mom hasn't actually used it since his dad left in 1982. She just likes to fill it with junk.

But we're still laughing.

"You wrote that yourself, girl," says Jos, still giggling and wiping tears.

"I didn't; I swear I didn't."

Brodie covers his head with a beach towel, then gets up.

"I'm going for a swim," he says. Then he steps in the wading pool.

"Love don't last forever," I say.

"For real," Jos grunts, and Brodie keeps pretending he's swimming in the Pacific.

16

CURTIS IS STILL ASLEEP WHEN I LEAVE FOR school—on a Sunday. I lay my head on his smooth back and listen to him breathing for a minute. Then I'm out the door speeding down country roads, 'cause I'm going to be late.

It's too hot to be inside today—but here we all are. It's too hot to think about a future doing this or doing that. Too hot . . .

I watch Brodie as he leans against the gym wall and starts to read pamphlets he's picked up from the tables. The halls are packed. And I don't want to be here. But I've got to get my slip signed by at least three of the people sitting behind tables trying to convince a whole group of sleepy kids that they want to have careers.

Marley walks over with a cup of coffee in her hand.

"How ya been?"

And that "How ya been?" is really about ten questions but she lets it slide when I answer.

"Okay."

Okay.

She puts her arm around me, and we lean on each other while we decide what fake careers we want to be interested in.

I'm thinking I want to be a fake veterinarian. Or even a fake IT person. Marley thinks she wants to be a fake college dropout and make her parents real proud. I look for Brodie, but he's gone. I wonder what fake career he's getting to snag enough signatures.

I give it up after my fake career as a vet is busted up before I even get started.

Allergies. But at least the woman signed my slip.

We walk around eating popcorn—free. Drinking pop—not free—until I see Brodie off in a corner sitting next to two men in uniforms. Their hair is crew cut and their shoes shine under the fluorescent lights. Even though it's warm, their jackets stay on, and they look crisp and cool. Too cool.

But it's not just Brodie. There's about ten boys that I know all sitting around and listening like they never listen to anything else.

I wonder how they got in.

Then I imagine I see the darkest eyes ever. Was he one of these boys not so long ago? Probably.

There are tear streaks.

First it's hot and a summer day.

And then I see the darkest eyes . . .

The darkest eyes.

I sit in front of the army recruiting office after leaving the career fair, and the sun is so hot I think I'm gonna pass out. I should just take my ass back to the woods and Curtis—but here I am. There's a glare coming off the windshield, and I have to tilt my head a certain way to get a good look at the recruiting office.

I lean across the seat and pop the glove compartment. I burn myself on the hinge, then pull out a pair of Curtis's aviator sunglasses. They slide down my nose. I turn on the radio and wait.

There are only so many locks in the world, but most of them are no match for somebody who knows an Angry Goth Boy who knows someone who has keys to get in any building downtown.

Thanks, Angry Goth Boy.

I drag the plastic garbage bag full of army brochures, pens, and blank notepaper through the alley behind the bank. Everybody uses the alleys between the stores downtown as shortcuts coming from school. I know every turn. I know the easiest ways and the nearest escapes (from skipping class with Carl).

The best Dumpster this time is at Singing Sam's Pizza.

I make sure nobody sees or hears me while I drag the bag past the back door and want pizza— but I have to finish this. Right now. I throw it in the Dumpster, change my mind about pizza, and walk back to Alice.

The sun isn't as hot when I turn on some old Tupac, push the sunglasses back up, and head back to the woods and Curtis.

17

THAT FIRST NIGHT I LIVED IN THE CABIN
with Curtis, I slept all alone. After I turned Alice
toward the gap in the trees, I slept in the big bed
with the scary wooden gargoyles carved on the
ends of the headboard, my box of jeans beside
me on the floor. Curtis gave me hot chamomile
tea, then took a blanket from a wooden chest
at the foot of the bed and went to sleep on the
couch.

I still don't know why he let me stay.

I gotta admit he was the only person I had
ever even looked at. He had the darkest eyes. I
loved him. I already knew it.

I loved him the day I dropped that big-assed
box of T-shirts at Jos's and he was buying wings

for his sister. I didn't think I'd ever see him again after he and his family moved away and left their house stone empty.

I looked.

Everybody did, 'cause they just seemed to disappear.

But that day I dropped a big-assed box on my foot, Curtis helped Jos ice my foot, and all I wanted to do was touch his beautiful brown face. And I almost did. But it felt too crazy—even for me.

His T-shirt said HIRAM COLLEGE and the only thing he said to me was, "You okay?"

After they put ice on my foot, he took his wings and left.

If you asked me now, I'd say we just ran into each other accidentally.

If asked now, I'd say that's just the way it was supposed to be.

We sat next to each other in a movie—Brodie, Marley, and Butchy on the one side of me. And three guys with Hiram colors on the other side of him.

I smiled and he asked about my foot.

Then he gave me a dollar at the carnival to win Butchy a kangaroo that I swore looked just like him. Butchy, that is. I was fishing for change, and there he was. Then he was gone.

Later he was buying birdseed at the hardware store when I came in looking for two-sided tape to put a poster up.

Our last run-in was when he pulled alongside me on the road when Alice decided to run out of gas.

He said, "If you're okay to come to my house, I live up the road. I think I have enough gas to get you and your truck home. Or stay here and I'll be back in a minute."

I'm not crazy—even though he had the darkest eyes, that didn't mean he wasn't a serial killer.

I waited.

He smiled, left, disappeared into some trees and bushes about one hundred yards up the road, and came back a few minutes later with gas. We were both happy that Alice was so old she wasn't fuel-injected and needed a gas station.

As I pulled away he said, "Good night, Sweet."

And I said, "Later, Curtis."

Curtis loved to sit in an old rocking chair and read books on the porch of the cabin. He said his uncle stayed here when he was hunting; now the place belongs to Curtis. When it got dark, he brought out candles—and at first the only thing I was thinking was he was going to mess up his eyes and would go blind. . . . (Does every thing your mama says stick?)

But soon enough when I got home from Jos's or from school, I'd be on the cabin porch with or without him—reading.

And I didn't go hungry, 'cause I ate whatever he put in front of me.

Reading and eating—that's mostly what we did in the beginning.

One night might be corn on the cob with lots of melted butter and black pepper, sliced tomatoes, and some Lake Erie fish he'd bought from some man up the road with an ice chest and fishing lures all over him.

Another night it might be sweet corn bread, red beans and rice with sweet onions, and sun tea—honey sweetened. I'd watched him from the window shirtless and barefoot take the huge canning jar out one morning, fill it, and put it in a sunny spot by the wild roses.

But the dinner I remember most was the wild salad filled with fruit and nuts and some kind of sweet creamy dressing that made me want to eat it by the bowlful. Then we crunched crusty bread that was moist and buttery inside— Curtis talked about poetry and fishing.

That night, after eighteen nights, we shared the big bed, and I fell asleep next to him.

This poem fell out of a book about the history of the buffalo soldiers.

I am too young to have gone
to seven funerals this past year.
I have stopped wearing black
because the Ohio heat
rips through me to
cook me to
the bone.

Three classmates at one time
nine months ago
when their car flipped over.
Three
separate
funerals.
A cousin's heart gave out in front
of his whole family.
Graveside
services
only.

A girl who was my
first crush
lost a brother
to the pipe.
They had to carry
her mom out the church.

And during a cold
snap one of our
neighbors slept
forever because of a faulty
heater.

And I thought that
would be the end
of it all.
Death
and said so to my
grandma.
But she looked at me with red eyes
that said
it
was
only
the beginning.

ANGELA JOHNSON

18

CURTIS LOVES TO WALK THROUGH THE woods. But I have a fever and don't think I can make this walk. Earlier, all I wanted to do was curl up on the bathroom floor and feel the cool of the toilet bowl just as I was about to throw up again. I got to know the bathroom real good.

Curtis stood outside the door and every few minutes asked how I was doing.

I didn't answer. Didn't have to.

He could hear me hurl, and I guess that was enough for him to know I was still alive.

At first he'd shadowed me. He stood behind me to make sure I didn't fall in the toilet. But after my second dive—even I got to be embarrassed that he was seeing me in the toilet bowl.

You'd think being that kind of sick would make a person lose all kind of modesty—a word I learned from my mom, but not usually in my dictionary.

Not so.

Curtis was still walking around upright 'cause he didn't go "old-food-in-the-refrigerator diving" with me. I didn't eat anything green or blue, but I guess I was off by a week or so about how old some of it was.

Even though I still feel sick as a dog, I go into the woods with Curtis anyway.

His arms are wrapped around my shoulders while I suck water out of a bottle and hope he'll walk slow. He does—and keeps asking if I should be resting. He could show me what he wanted to later, when I feel better (which is to say when I'm too empty to throw up anymore). I now take the walk as a dare and say so.

He laughs.

We walk over fallen trees and go off the path by the creek. Most of the underbrush is mossy from lack of sunshine.

I'm starting to feel a bit better.

Don't want to throw up at all now.

We keep walking, though—and I squeeze his hand hard and look up through the leaves on

ANGELA JOHNSON

the trees. I can see the sun trying to shine down through them. The trees look damned tall as I gaze up, but we go farther in the woods, and it gets darker and cooler, until finally I can't hear the creek or any crickets.

The woods are as quiet as the first minutes of sleep.

But I am with Curtis, his hand around mine, when the old wooden shack appears between two old oaks. I look at Curtis, but I never ask why we're here. It ain't like me.

Scares me when I think about how much I sometimes think not like me anymore.

But I trust him, and being sick doesn't help. Maybe I'm just too damned tired to question as we stand outside the old wooden shack with the flat roof. Wildflowers grow around it—tiny flowers that appear purple in the twilight. Curtis opens the door and pulls me into the dirt-floor shack—I look around and step back out. Curtis follows me.

"It's an old storage shack. My pops's friends used to keep their extra rifles locked up in here when they were out in the woods."

"I like it. It reminds me of the cabin, only miniature."

The moon streams down through a clearing in the trees and comes down right beside the little shack. Curtis pulls a blanket out of his pack and puts it down against a wall so I can lean against it. Then he sits down beside me. I lean against him, and he feels my forehead.

"Ooh—fever germs," he says.

I rub my face against his. "A few sick cooties for you . . ."

Curtis closes his eyes.

"I dreamed about this, ya know."

"You dreamed about me having a fever and you dragging me into the woods to an old storage shack?"

"No, no. I dreamed about coming back here when I was over there."

"Oh," I say.

"I dreamed of rain, pine trees, and these woods. Sometimes I almost started to think that real color didn't exist anymore. I mean, you don't see wildflowers like these in the desert."

He runs his hands over the carpet of purple flowers surrounding us and the shack. Curtis barely ever wants to talk about Iraq, so I listen quietly.

"I dreamed about sitting on the porch. I dreamed about the quiet. I don't think I've ever missed this quiet so much. The quiet of birds chirping and midnight train whistles. There was another kind of quiet in Iraq. A quiet I never got used to.

"And sometimes you could almost feel when something was gonna happen. I mean, you knew. You felt it coming."

I want to ask him if he was scared most of the time—but I stop myself, because I figure it's a stupid question. Who wouldn't be scared with people trying to kill them?

So I just say— "You need to stay home and sit on your porch."

Curtis gets up and starts pacing in front of me; then I guess he remembers where he is and sits down to soak in the woods and the quiet.

"I don't want to go back, but if I have to—I have to. It's me or some other poor fool."

"Why can't it be nobody?" I say.

Curtis feels my head.

"Are you delusional?"

"No—just hopeful and pissed, I guess."

Curtis laughs, but I've seen him happier, or maybe I really am delusional.

He lies back on the blanket, and I sprinkle grass on him.

"I dreamed about this. I really dreamed about just being here, and it was perfect, just like it is now. I don't want anything else. No food, no house. I just want to be here. It's perfect, Sweet. I could die here just like this."

19

WHEN CURTIS STARTED SCREAMING IN HIS
sleep, it was like the end of the world.

At first he would just breathe hard in his sleep.
Usually it would stop there. Or he'd wake himself
up. But mostly it was just the breathing hard.

I'd watch him until his breath slowed.

It was no big deal at first. Just a dream.
Maybe a nightmare.

But then the screaming started, and on
top of that it looked like he was trying to carry
something in his hand. All I could do was try to
wake him up. It was hard to do that. Especially
with him screaming for people to stop or run or
help him take something away.

When he finally did wake up, he'd complain
that his arms hurt.

He'd say— "Man—my arms are sore."

Then he'd look over at me next to him like he was asking me if I knew the reason. And I could have told him that it looked to me that in his dream he was always trying to pick something up.

I could have told him that, but I didn't.

I didn't, because I wouldn't have been able to stop there. I would have wanted to know when the dreams started and were they because of something that happened over there in Iraq (which he never wanted to talk about). So when he finally tries to get to sleep again, this time I just lie beside him and stare into the dark until I only hear his slow breathing and the creek outside.

I should ask him about the nightmares.

But I don't think that will keep them away. And when it comes to bad dreams, all anybody ever wants is for them to stay away.

A letter from my mama:

Sweet,

I wanted to send you this on your birthday, but it didn't seem like something you would appreciate. I haven't really found that thing, have I? But I promise, I think about you all the time. You are never out of my mind.

I know that you are still going to school and working at your friend's store. I know because I check up on you. I have not left you completely.

But I knew I had to let you go. You've been leaving since you were born. I could never put my arms around you enough to get you to stay. I guess I could have continued forcing you like I have been doing all these years. But I can't do that anymore. You have made up your mind.

I trust that you are happier where you are than you were with us.

Are you?

Are you understood? Do you laugh more? Does this young man

make you know that you are
loved?

Everyone, your father included,
thinks I'm crazy for not dragging
you back. But they don't
understand. You'd run further
and faster. At least this way you
are within my heart's reach. And
my hands if they might be helpful
or needed.

Do you drive by the house? I
think I see you sometimes.

Do you? I hope so.

Maybe one day you will drop by,
come in, or just come back. . . .

    Love,

    Mama

Come and Gone

20

I GAVE BUTCHY A RIDE HOME FROM school and talked to Marley for a few minutes, then—'cause Marley said he'd asked about me—drove over to Bobby's to check out him and Feather. It was a good day.

I even stopped and talked to my brother Jason, who was coming out of the drugstore. I pulled over and opened Alice's door for him to get in and talk a bit. And to save my life I don't know what we talked about.

But it made me happy as I drove on back to the woods and Curtis. And when I got back to Curtis and the cabin, the place smelled good. Food was cooking, and Curtis was smiling and singing as I put my car keys on top of an official-looking opened envelope.

I got a twinge 'cause I was so happy right then. I got a twinge 'cause I was feeling a little guilty. I never told Curtis about the soldiers who showed up. Maybe he knows, though. Maybe he saw them coming. Maybe he watched them and me from the woods. He's not a fool. He knows he's AWOL. But I don't want to break everything up now.

I just can't.

Curtis had put on some zydeco music I'd never heard but liked a lot.

He kept looking at me. Dark-eyed. Dark-eyed and smiling.

Every now and then he'd remember the groundhog bowl and put vegetable peels in it.

"So what do you want for dinner?" he asked.

"Whatever you got in the oven or on the stove," I laughed. He always asked. I'd eat the wood off the side of the cabin if somebody put cheese on it. I love to eat.

We ate, talked, and laughed. And after that I helped him clear the table and wash the dishes. When we were done, we sat on the couch entwined and listened to the woods.

There were long arms all around me, and I just knew I was going to get in trouble for not getting home. Then I remembered this was home and fell back to sleep. When I woke up again, he wasn't there.

I looked everywhere in the cabin, then out in the yard.

I was barefoot and felt the chill.

But I decided to keep looking for him.

It's pitch dark in the woods when I finally come out. My feet are so cold it's like they aren't even attached to me as I watch them scratched and bleeding. And if I looked in a mirror, I know my hair would be full of leaves and who knows what.

I walk through the front door and drop the flashlight on the couch.

I remember the groundhogs and take their scraps out to them. I feel like I'm sleepwalking, though.

The couch is calling me, 'cause I know I can't sleep in the bed. I ache.

I decide I'll ache on the couch or maybe not in the cabin at all. When I walk over to the table to get my keys, I knock all the mail off, and a letter floats to my feet from the army.

I read it, drop it, then curl up on the couch and listen to the leaves blowing in the breeze outside and think about how I feel that I might never be warm again but don't have the strength to go get a blanket.

When I wake the sun is dragging itself from behind some clouds, and there's a blanket around me, but in my heart I know I am all alone, even if I can't remember if I covered myself in the first place.

21

BRODIE ISN'T IN CLASS TODAY. EVERYBODY is saying it has something to do with cops and career day. And I think about my criminal activity on career day and wonder what Brodie might have done.

I don't even want to start guessing. Everybody in this school is so bored they make up half the stuff they say. But I do start to wonder where Brodie is. I miss him at lunch when no one comes up and eats half the bad food that's on my tray.

I miss him in Jameson's class, 'cause I don't have anybody to pass notes to or egg on to disrupt the class before I pass out from boredom. Angry Goth Boy has been a real disappointment lately.

Maybe he's on medication. He wears a lot less black.

Lately.

Too bad.

It's sad to see a body stop raging into the dying of any light.

Sorry, Angry Goth Boy.

The halls have emptied out for fourth period, and I'm late as usual when I see Brodie walking slow down the other end of the hall. I wave to him, then slide down against my locker to wait for him. In about a minute he's sitting next to me on the floor.

"I'm heading to the store," I say.

Brodie takes off his sunglasses.

"Good I saw you before you broke out. . . ."

He takes a banana out of his shoulder bag, starts to peel it, then offers me a bite.

I say, "Nope—too banana."

He snorts.

I snort back.

"So what's up with everybody talking about something happening to you with career day?"

"Damn! These people must have spies on every corner." Brodie jumps up and looks under his arms. "Do I got bugs on me or what?"

I smile, and he sits back down beside me.

"What do you have to kill around here to get a little privacy?"

"Boredom," I say.

Brodie nods and finishes his banana.

"So why you creepin' in?"

He puts the peel back into his bag and fishes out an apple and a bottle of orange juice. He takes a swig of juice and starts laughing.

"The cops, the army, and my old man."

"Oh, shit, Brodie—you didn't join, did you?"

Brodie doesn't say a word. He just sits there eating his apple and drinking. When he's done, he takes his sunglasses out of his bag, puts them on, and stares at me.

"Ya know, Sweet girl, it's like you don't know me at all. . . ."

Then he gets up and smiles down at me and says—

"You should find a better Dumpster than the pizza parlors. I'd find something more toward the township."

I look up at him.

Then Brodie walks toward class, turns around, shrugging, and yells—

"I'm just saying . . ."

And it's like I don't know him all over again—but like him more than almost anybody.

When I finally get to bed tonight, I listen to the creek and imagine the groundhogs underneath the cabin. I listen for Curtis, who hasn't been back since the night I read the letter from the army. . . .

Now when I come home from work and school I go for walks along the edge of the woods, cook because I want to get used to it, or get in Alice and drive around town.

Sometimes I go by Jos's house and listen to him and his mother annoy each other after he's closed the store.

Yesterday I hung out with his mother, Willa, who makes me laugh and is a whole lot more crazy than anyone I've ever met.

She yells for me to come in when I knock and ask if Jos is home.

"Come on in, honey. Jos went to Cleveland to pick up something from a supplier. Some woman who makes charms or something—I don't know."

I walk into the living room, and she's knitting.

There's yarn—everywhere.

Jos's mom has a graying curly Afro, weighs about eighty pounds, and is what my mom would call a serious hippie chick. But I wouldn't say that. I think she's living in the here and now even though Jos was born in a commune.

"Sit, kid," she says, and pushes about twenty balls of yarn out of the butterfly chair.

So I just sit and watch her knit.

"Tea," she says after a while, and I say, "I'll get it"—and do.

Willa puts down her knitting and starts drinking her tea.

"Good tea, kid."

"Thanks."

Then she stares at me for a long time. Jos told me way before I met her that she was always trying to see inside people's souls. Freaky.

"You happy?"

Okay—that shit shocks me, 'cause I was just thinking how I wasn't. . . . I don't want to lie, so I say, "Sometimes."

She picks up her knitting again. "Well, sometimes—sometimes has to be enough."

"I always thought so," I say.

"Maybe you ought to go back home. Maybe you miss your family."

I say, "Maybe." And then think about my

brothers at home. "But I don't think so—I'm all right where I am."

Willa nods her head and turns to look out the window.

"Well, from everything I've heard, you'll be okay with that Wright boy. Knew his family before they left for parts unknown. Nice. And he seems lovely and sincere."

I take a roll of yarn in my hand and start squeezing it.

"Have you ever met him?"

Willa laughs. "As a matter of fact he drove me and a couple of my friends to a demonstration out by the campus. Parking was gonna be a mess, and we didn't want to get towed. He overheard a few of my girlfriends and me in the coffee shop talking. He offered to take us, 'cause he had a parking permit. He actually drove us there in his uniform and was waiting for us by his car when it was all over.

"Amazing young man. Lovely, sad, but amazing."

I squeeze the soft pink yarn harder.

"Yes, yes he —is. . . ."

She stares at me again while I start to wrap the yarn around my fingers.

In and around.

After a while Willa starts talking about her volunteer work and how impossible it is to get anything organic in Heaven after the summer vegetable stands close up. And she's really sick of having to haul ass to another cute overpriced market in one of the rich suburbs.

I feel warm and safe when she talks, and I pour myself more tea and get lost in her world of feeding the homeless, antiwar protests, and the never-ending quest for food that won't eventually kill you. I like Willa. And when she talks about anything and everything, it smoothes over the fact that I will have to go back to a place that I love—but that is quiet and lonely.

Lonely and quiet.

And it's going to be that way until it isn't anymore.

The evening sun starts to go down while I listen to the calm and Willa.

22

So the story is (and everybody thinks they know it by now) that I either ran away or was kicked out of my parents' house for drugs, drinking, being pregnant, or—if you listen to the most messed-up story—all of them. After all these months of living in the cabin people just now are asking what happened! And when it looks like somebody is going to ask me, I just stare right through 'em and dare them to ask.

Nobody has so far.

So the bullshit just keeps rolling down the hill, and I don't do anything to stop it.

Why?

Why not?

Curtis says people like to be knee-deep in it anyway.

I say it makes 'em feel better about their boring lives when they think of a tragic one for somebody else. We love to hear the tragic stories. The news is full of them, and it makes me feel good that I live where I never have to watch it.

And when I'm just walking around the cabin in one of Curtis's old shirts, going window to window—I miss that he was here. His smell. His touch.

Him.

Maybe Willa is right about me going home, but then I walk to a shelf and pull out a book and get lost in it and I don't have to think about anything else.

The story is about a girl alone in the woods who left home 'cause she couldn't be happy there no matter how she or anybody else tried to make it so.

I go window to window, and the story never changes.

To the Bone

23

CURTIS HAS NOT COME HOME. THE woods did not give him up the night I almost froze looking for him. But who do I tell? What do I do? In a breath you can be gone from this place—anyplace. And the only thing you leave behind is what you meant to someone.

Curtis hardly ever talks—but the night that he left, he talked more than I'd ever heard him before. Was it a gift?

The first few days I went to school and tried not to think about it. I believed he'd be back. Quiet and sad, maybe, but he'd be back. He is not back, and maybe after a while I'll have to do something else to look for him.

· · ·

For a long time—there were no caskets. Not one. Not one to be photographed, not one to 'cause pain, not one to make people remember.

Where were the caskets?

I want all the yellow ribbons to disappear off of big-assed SUVs.

I want people to stop waving flags like it makes them better than people who don't.

I want never to hear one more word about being patriotic—'cause most of them don't even know what the hell patriotism is.

I want to sit in class and not think that some of the people around me might end up shooting or getting shot at by people they'd never know.

The new president now says we can see the caskets come home.

Good.

What if everybody starts forgetting that people are dying again, even with the caskets?

What if everybody fuckin' forgets?

Because there are caskets now, and people still forget.

And what if everybody just starts paying attention to something else and never cares 'cause they've never taken the time to see the caskets?

24

BRODIE AND JOS TAKE TO THE COURT after seven little elementary kids in a pickup game finish fighting over their basketball for about the hundredth time. All three of us were leaning against the fence and laughing until about a minute ago, when Brodie took the basketball and shot it up into the tree overhanging the court.

Damn—little kids shouldn't cuss—but Jos and Brodie just laugh harder at them while they wait for their ball to fall. It doesn't, and they finally give up waiting. A couple of them are still talking smack as they walk away down the sidewalk.

I take a couple of free shots and make all of them, but then lose interest and let Brodie and

Jos have the ball they brought to the court with them.

A few minutes after they start playing, the other basketball finally falls out of the tree and rolls toward me on the other side of the court. I think about chasing the kids to give it back but change my mind, get up, and hide it behind the weeds by the tree.

Maybe they'll think about looking over there if they come back.

It's hard to lose things.

"So what's it about, anyway? Except for the obvious," Brodie says after making about twenty one-handed layups and jogging around the court.

I know he's talking to me, 'cause Jos stopped playing about a half hour ago and is reading a graphic novel now with his iPod probably turned high enough to make him deaf for a couple of days.

Brodie sits down on the court beside me.

I smile. "Do we ever talk to each other in chairs anymore?"

Brodie throws the basketball up in the air and lets it roll off the court. "True dat . . ."

"So what do you wanna know?"

Brodie stretches his legs out.

"Crimes, girl. Crimes against military brochures, locks, military premises."

"It wasn't that much. But how come you know so much? You moved too fast the other day to tell me anything."

"Somebody saw me in the neighborhood around the time you committed your little civil disobedience."

"Why were you there?"

"Hangin' out."

"Downtown—on a Sunday. Everything is closed."

"Uh-huh."

I look at Brodie and finally get it.

"You were following me?"

"Damn, Sweet, sometimes you are seriously slow. I worry about you—a lot lately. You're in some kind of daze. Where you at?"

"Fine—I'm okay Brodie."

"Just fine—or okay?" he says.

"You are getting on my nerves now."

Brodie just nods at me, then walks over to the basketball and shoots it one-handed. I remember the summer he wore his right hand in a sling so he could learn how to shoot left-handed. He's good any way he shoots now.

Jos is still reading and ignoring us.

Brodie pops a few from the corner a few times, then moves back far enough for three points and makes it. Then he goes to the free-throw line and shoots until he misses.

The sun's starting to go down, and in a minute the street-lights will start coming on. I hear somebody's mother calling them down the street, a dog barking, and a car starting up across the road from the courts. It's all the sounds I didn't think I would ever miss after moving out to the woods. But I do—sometimes now.

Just sometimes.

Jos closes his book, takes out his earphones in time enough for Brodie to ask, "Where is he, Sweet? Where's your boy Curtis?"

I CLEANED THE CABIN FROM TOP TO bottom the day after Curtis left. I mean, I didn't just clean it; I scrubbed it. Hard. With an old scrub brush I found under the kitchen sink that looked about a hundred years old.

I used soap, bleach, pine cleaner. Anything I could find.

I called Jos and told him I was sick. I never miss work. I could mess it all up, missing anything about school—even though me and Jos are cool. Sometimes the school checks your vocational employers. They just show up.

I scrubbed the floors.

The walls.

The bathroom.

I scrubbed the front porch, too.

Everything in me told me he wasn't coming back. I just knew it. I knew it 'cause he was disappearing every day that I was there and had probably started way before I ever left home. And anyway, he'd never promised me anything—just a home for a while. That's it.

We hadn't known each other long enough to love each other.

And I hadn't known him well enough, period.

So I scrubbed until my hands felt raw to the bone.

And even though I'd dream about his arms and eyes and sometimes forget he was gone and imagine that I heard him—I knew.

I knew he was gone forever.

Brodie and Jos read the letter from the army, and there's this part of me says that the letter is private, meant only for Curtis. Or his family. But they aren't here. They're all in Texas now.

"So they were sending him back." Jos is shaking his head.

I walk over to the couch, sit, and look out the window.

Brodie says, "I guess in a while they'll

be sending out the MPs to get him for going AWOL—huh?"

"He's not AWOL," I say.

Brodie and Jos look at me, then at the letter again.

It's the first time I've let anybody in the cabin since Curtis left. I thought anybody would be able to tell like I did that he was gone. It no longer smells or feels like he ever lived here. I mean—there are his books and music, but those could belong to anybody.

"Where do you think he went, Sweet?" Jos asks, then walks across the room and sits next to me on the couch.

I point toward the woods.

"Have you looked?" He asks.

I don't say I don't have the nerves to go back into the woods.

Brodie stands with his arms folded, staring out the window.

"It's been pretty cool at night lately."

Jos must know what he's talking about, 'cause he stands up and walks over to Brodie.

"We'll be back, okay."

"Just stay here and try to get some rest."

"Don't worry—we got this."

And in a minute they're both gone.

I watch the door closing and am left sitting on the couch looking out the window at a quiet, sunny day while Brodie and Jos go into the woods.

I walk over and take a CD from the shelf, put it in the stereo, and listen to zydeco for a little while.

Hereafter

26

I LOOK AT THE FRONT PAGE OF THE
newspaper now and see Jos standing by the
cop looking like an old man. They didn't take
a picture of Brodie (or they did and just didn't
use it).

Nobody knows it, but I was hiding in the
bushes, 'cause in the end I'd listened to enough
music and decided to go into the woods to look
for them. They weren't in Curtis's grandpa's
woods. So I kept walking.

The sun was high and hot when I finally
found them, cops and EMS on the edge of the
woods and blocking Route 306, about a mile
past the cabin. They were loading a body into

an ambulance. Jos shook his head, and the cop reached over and touched his arm.

That's when the photographer aimed her camera.

And I walked back through the woods.

27

CURTIS'S FAMILY WILL FLY HIS BODY BACK to Texas. One of his older brothers, Jules, came from Texas to take him back to his family.

I got to see Curtis at the morgue because I begged. I wasn't family, and he'd already been identified. But I begged as my mother stood beside me—this time. She held my hand as we walked into the room.

The day before Jules leaves with Curtis, he comes to the cabin. I am waiting for him. I have been waiting since the day Curtis found out he had to go back to Iraq, then knew he couldn't. I've been waiting for his family.

I'm sitting on the porch. My duffel bag is packed inside when he pulls up in what must be a rental. He's wearing a black suit and dark glasses. He takes the glasses off when he walks up the steps.

His eyes look just like Curtis's.

"Sweet?"

"Yes."

"I remember you from the old neighborhood."

I smile 'cause I can't cry anymore.

"Jules," he says, while putting his hand out for me to shake.

I do and look in his eyes.

He walks into the cabin and starts walking from room to room. Slowly and like a stranger who's never been there.

"He loved this place. He was the only one in the family who did."

Jules breathes out and starts looking at Curtis's books and music—then shakes his head.

"Did you take what you wanted?" he asks me.

"I don't need anything," I say, then hold out the key.

He looks at the key, hands me a piece of paper, then turns away and heads out the door.

"Keep it. And if you don't mind, we'll need someone to check on the cabin every now and then—if you can and don't mind."

I put the key in my back jean pocket and nod my head and read his address and phone number in Texas. In a minute he's disappeared down the driveway and out onto the road. I walk through the cabin again, only not like Jules. I know this place.

I remember the man who lived here and took me into this safe place—for a while. Then left me here when he couldn't feel safe anymore.

I sit on the front porch until the sun starts to go down. I take my bags, toss them in the back of Alice, start her up, then slowly drive through the trees.

I look back just as the first groundhog of the night comes out.

The poem Jules put in Curtis's coffin for me:

In the sweet hereafter
everything
that you ever wanted
in your heart
will float to your
feet.

In the sweet hereafter
everyone that you know
will know who you
are.
And your heart
will be an open book.

In the sweet hereafter
there will be no
bombs,
grenades,
IEDS,
needlessly dead
or perpetually dying boys, girls,
men, women, and babies.

In the sweet hereafter there will be
no reason—no reason at all.

ANGELA JOHNSON

LIFE. LOVE. FRIENDSHIP.

From critically acclaimed author Ellen Wittlinger.

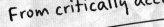

Love & Lies

Hard Love

Parrotfish

Heart on My Sleeve

Blind Faith

Razzle

Sandpiper

SIMON & SCHUSTER BFYR

TEEN.SimonandSchuster.com